North's Pole

Written by Lindsay Yacovino
and Courtney D'Annunzio

Illustrated by Kaitlyn Terrey

To our children, may the spirit of Christmas always be in your hearts—L.Y. & C.D.

www.onelittlesparkpublishing.com

To request permission, write to
One Little Spark Publishing, 24 Valerie Lane, Hamilton, NJ 08690.

ISBN 978-1-7378820-0-8 (paperback)
ISBN 978-1-7378820-2-2 (ebook)
ISBN 978-1-7378820-1-5 (hardcover)

Library of Congress Number: 2021918354

2 4 6 8 10 9 7 5 3 1
First edition

One little spark publishing

In Santa's Christmas Village, all young elves will learn their role.
They're taught by North herself—through special classes at North's Pole.
To help the elves get started, North consults a detailed list—
a page for every elf-job! But, this year, there's quite a twist.

She greets the ten new elves while giving smiles to everyone—
then double-checks their jobs and sees one elf was given none!

As North is 'taking roll,' each name and job are closely paired.
Left standing all alone is Tess—appearing very scared.

"Without a job assigned to me,
what elf will I become?
And should I pick my favorite?
Or perhaps just sample some?"

With North by Tess's side, they'll surely figure out this test.
"We'll try each job together; then, we'll choose what fits you best."

So, North and Tess begin with what is every Elfie's dream:
Creating sweets all day as part of Santa's Twisting Team.

Soon, Tess is watching Cooper, Twister of the Candy Canes.
He's quickly curling sticks of mint, as Head-Elf North explains.

And then, it's Tess's turn to make a classic taffy twist.
Instead of canes of candy, she has knots around her wrist.

The skill of bending treats might simply not be meant for Tess.
"These candy canes are great— But I don't like this twisty mess!"

Then, North reminds her elf, "You only need one perfect match.
We've got more stops to go. So, next, we'll try to bake from scratch!"
Then, Tess and North will follow all the smells of baking sweets.
And Tess can do a 'baking test' to join the Shoppe of Treats.

Across from Tess is Grady, Baker of The Gingerbread.

"I'm so excited," Tess declares. "Let's bake a Christmas spread!"

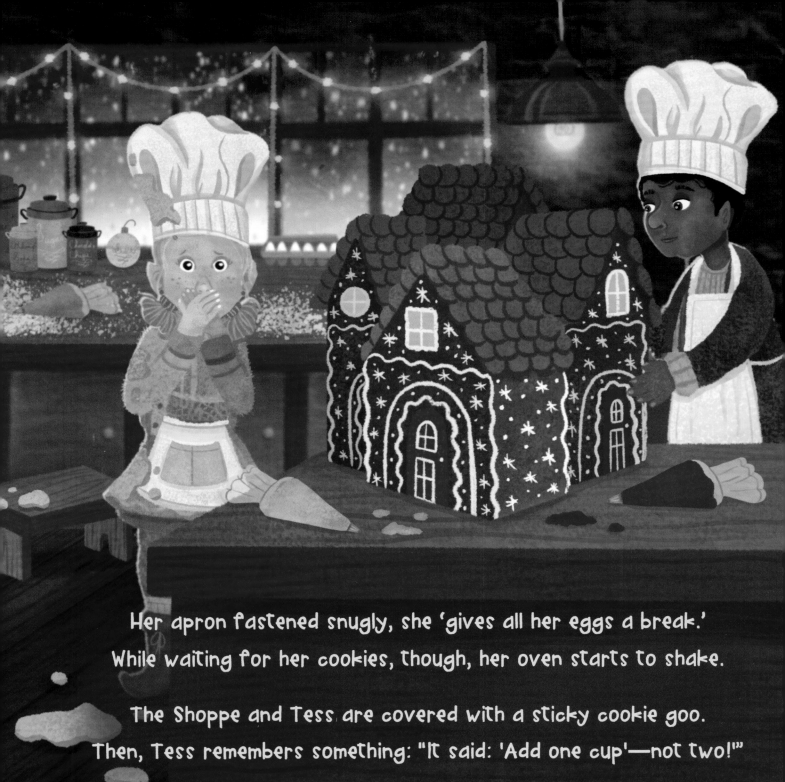

Her apron fastened snugly, she 'gives all her eggs a break.'
While waiting for her cookies, though, her oven starts to shake.

The Shoppe and Tess are covered with a sticky cookie goo.
Then, Tess remembers something: "It said: 'Add one cup'—not two!'"

To twist and bake desserts may not be every Elfie's niche.
So, North suggests to Tess, "I think perhaps you're meant to stitch."

The sound of Elf-like giggles
from The Stitchery, they hear.
It's where the underwear is sewn
and stored in heaps—each year.

The Bakery

The newest seamstress Emme, Stitcher of The Underwear,
has speedy sewing skills that maybe Tess will come to share.

One underwear design has polka dots and shiny thread.
Tess sews a nice pink undie, which adorns her dress instead.

"I guess I'm not for sewing undies!" says a laughing Tess.
And North is smiling with her—at the funny messed-up dress.

"Come, Tess—I have a new idea that just might work for you.
Let's go to Santa's Workshop, where you'll hammer, build, and glue."

The sound of tap-tap-tapping welcomes North and Tess inside.
And greeting Tess is Builder Ben, a first-rate building guide.

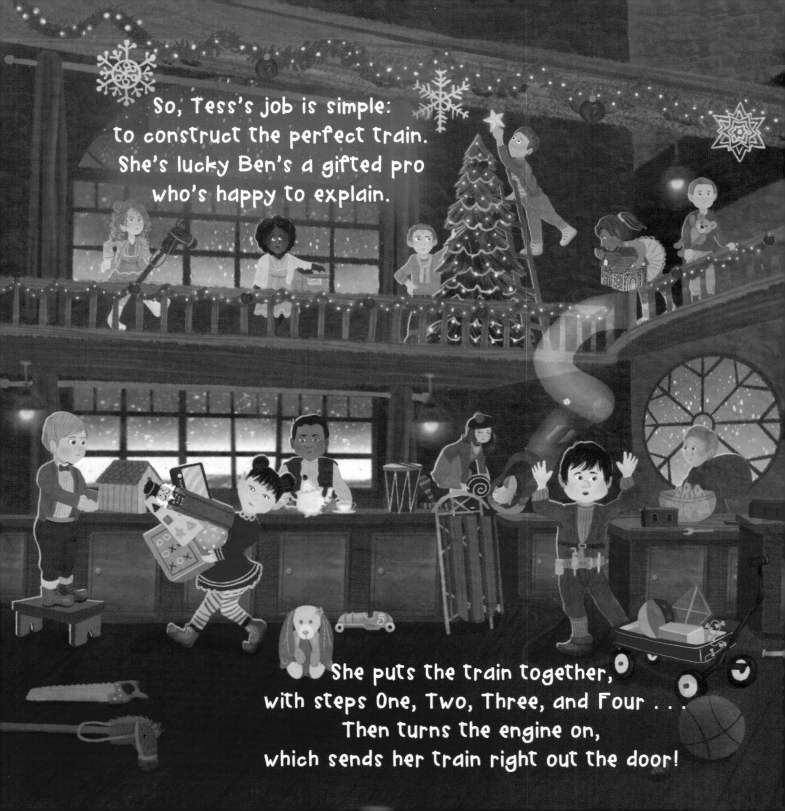

So, Tess's job is simple:
to construct the perfect train.
She's lucky Ben's a gifted pro
who's happy to explain.

She puts the train together,
with steps One, Two, Three, and Four . . .
Then turns the engine on,
which sends her train right out the door!

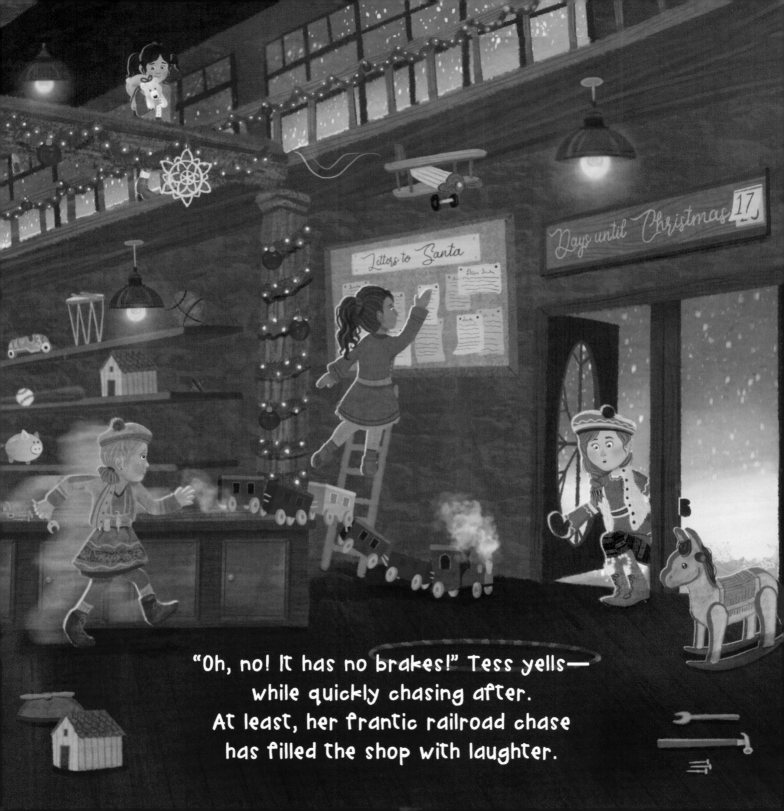

"Oh, no! It has no brakes!" Tess yells—
while quickly chasing after.
At least, her frantic railroad chase
has filled the shop with laughter.

This talent search is tough,
but North discovers what they need:
"Let's try the Lister Shop—
where all the elves just love to read."

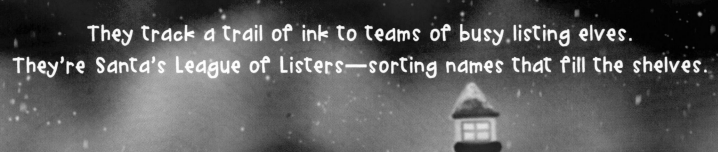

They track a trail of ink to teams of busy listing elves.
They're Santa's League of Listers—sorting names that fill the shelves.

There's List Inspector Lila who is checking A through C.
Like Tess, she's new today, but still,
she reads all day—with glee.

When Tess receives a page with D and E names on a list . . .
She checks the bad kids off as good; she simply can't resist.

It's good that Tess has North—and soon, 'eraser meets the page.'
"Perhaps it's best," says North to Tess, "to only check their age."

The elves just keep on listing—
Tess, by now, is grinning, too.
Remembering her friends,
she understands what she should do.

COOPER

GRADY

Among the piles of paper, she has found some crumpled wrap . . . And only minutes later, all her doodles fill each scrap.

BEN

LILA

EMME

Upon the wrapping, Tess has drawn the elves she met today—each face and name exactly right, in every single way.

When North returns, she finds
a happy elf who loves to draw.
It's Tess, who's sketching portraits,
leaving North to stare in awe.

Her special skill is clear,
and North has figured out her part.
"You're Tess the Tagging Elf!
You'll simply use your love of art!"

They travel 'round the Pole, where Tess will do her favorite thing.
She'll join the Tagging Troop, who love to tag the gifts and sing.

A stack of gifts is waiting, with some tags and markers, too . . .
for Tess, who's getting started making tags for kids like you.

She decorates each name-tag
with a holiday design—
then adds the perfect bow
and ties each one with stripy twine.

Since Tess has found her team, it seems that North has done her job.
She watches Tess embrace her role—then turns to grab the knob.
But just as North is leaving, Tagging Tess makes sure to say:
"I'm lucky you are Head-Elf North! I've found my Elfie way!"

It's time for North to leave—and go to help another elf.
Since, after all, it is her task to lead them all herself.

The sun begins to set,
and then it's North who says, "Goodnight."
"And welcome to North's Pole!" she adds.
"Sweet dreams to all! Sleep tight! "